Christmas comes but once a year...

but the spirit can last all year round.

Christmas Cowboys, Mistletoe Diner

and other Short Stories:

LARGE PRINT EDITION

A COLLECTION OF NEW FICTION FOR THE HOLIDAYS

Authors:
DIANNA BROWN
LARS DANIEL ERIKSSON
MICHAEL HABTE
SAMANTHA JAFFE
VIKRAM KALE
CHARLES KAMUYU
HAMEL MATTHEW
VALERIE SCOTT
LINDA SHAYNE
JIN A SONG
ALDO SPADONI
HOWARD STEINBERG

Edited by: MARILYN SINGLETON

Remember Point

Santa Monica, California

Published by Remember Point
P.O. Box 1448
Pacific Palisades, CA 90272

www.RememberPoint.com

ISBN-13: 978-1481127042
ISBN-10: 1481127047

Table of Contents

CHRISTMAS COWBOYS by Linda Shayne. 1

MISTLETOE DINER by Samantha Jaffe 10

CHANGE OF HEART by Vikram Kale 20

MISSILE DEFENSE AND SANTA TRACKING
    by Aldo Spadoni 32

MY CHRISTMAS ANGEL by Michael Habte . 37

SNOWBIRD by Valerie Scott 46

CHRISTMAS IN KENYA by Charles Kamuyu 56

TRIPLETS by Howard Steinberg. 65

CHRISTMAS TWISTER by Dianna Brown. . . 71

SECRET SANTA by Lars Daniel Eriksson. . . . 83

FOUR-DOOR IGLOO AND WOLVES
    by Jin A Song. 88

TRINIDAD by Hamel Matthew 91

ACKNOWLEDGEMENTS 95

CHRISTMAS COWBOYS

by Linda Shayne

Kendall's truck swerved dangerously on the black ice, hidden on the highway leading to Bose, Montana, a place she once called home. She turned on the radio in an attempt to calm her nerves. No one was crazy enough to drive five hundred miles in this weather, but it was Christmas Eve and her dad was waiting up for her, even though she was twenty-three.

A Garth Brooks country song provided some warmth and Kendall shifted into low gear to take the next curve at fifteen miles per. She always felt good when Garth's gravelly, velvet voice filled the air. Outside, rain turned to sleet and then snow.

Despite her better instincts, Kendall sped up; she had to pick up the pace or she would never make it home. Snow covered fields and flocked spruce trees glided by her in soft focus, as if she were in one of those 3-D movie theaters and wasn't wearing the required glasses.

The cold night had a surreal feel. Kendall's breath was visible and she tried to blow a series of steam rings, as she thought about how much had changed since she left home a year ago. She was different, just like everyone told her she would be if she moved to a big city like Houston. She was almost comfortable living in a concrete apartment building, she ate out at restaurants more often than she cooked, but she still hurt when she thought about her high school boyfriend and how he married her best friend's younger sister. He really was the reason she left town, that and there were no jobs in Bose.

When Kendall was approached by her

aunt's friend to sell medical equipment in Houston, she jumped at the chance to move. Living in a big city had its advantages. Shopping was incredible, there were sales almost every week, and her dating life was filled with guys wearing lab coats or suits and ties. Walking the halls of medical buildings, dressed in a skirt and heels peddling medical equipment was more effective than posting a profile on an internet dating site, but Kendall still felt disconnected. She missed her family and the rugged wilderness of Montana.

On the truck radio, a Carrie Underwood sound-alike came on and sang about rawhide and mistletoe. Kendall started singing along, feeling the country music Christmas spirit, when a deer bolted across the highway and froze in her headlights just a few feet ahead. Kendall slammed the brakes, turned the wheel and the truck skidded off the road. The deer ran off into the woods, as the truck whipped around, tipped over and landed hard on its side. The windshield cracked sharply like a sheet of thin ice.

Kendall didn't know how long she blacked out. When she awoke, she was partially twisted in her seatbelt, broken shards of glass glistened around her like diamonds. Somehow the radio still played on, a cowboy Christmas tune filled the air.

Kendall crawled out the driver's side window, more scared than harmed, but the cold wind caused her to shiver and she felt too shaken to stand. As she pushed her hands deeper into her jacket pockets searching for her cellphone, she found her old blue ski cap. She always wondered where she had misplaced it; she pulled it down on her head and was grateful for the warmth it provided.

The truck looked totaled and it was too far to even think about walking home. Kendall began to worry. She decided her best bet was to keep near the truck and stay alert for any car to drive by, although it was crazy to think anyone else was fool enough to drive the black ice that night. She gazed up at the almost full moon, trying to determine by its position how many more hours it would be until the sun rose, anything to keep her fear at bay.

The moon stared down on her. When Kendall was young, her mom would tell her that the moon was the eye of God watching over them. When Kendall asked where the other eye was, her mom replied that you couldn't see it, because God was winking. Then her mom would wink at her and Kendall knew everything would be alright. Her mom had passed away a few years ago, and now when Kendall looked up at the moon, she imagined it was her mom's eye watching over her. Kendall winked back and felt her mother's all encompassing love, and hearing her voice reassuring her that "this too shall pass."

A gentle snow began to fall. Through the gossamer layer of white, she noticed something moving faraway in the vast expanse. Kendall heard what she soon recognized as the sound of horses' hooves galloping across ice hard fields. She waved her arms and called out, but she wasn't sure she was heard.

The dawn was just about to break, the temperature was slowly rising and the curtain of snow dissolved. Like a mystical illusion, three cowboys on horseback appeared in silhouette on the distant horizon. They rode toward her and circled her before they stopped. One of the horses nuzzled her cold hand.

A cowboy slid off his horse and lifted Kendall into his saddle. He got on behind her and his warm breath whispered something soothing in her ear.

As they rode off, the sun broke through the clouds and they were surrounded by rays of golden light.

Kendall rode with the cowboys toward the hills. The exhilaration she felt as they galloped across the plains took her breath away, reawakening her soul, melting away all the heartache and pain she had been feeling.

The cowboys slowed the horses to a trot as they entered a narrow path in the foothills.

Snow covered pines formed a canopy over them. The cowboys rode single file; she was in the front, as the cowboy she was riding with took the lead.

When they came to a clearing at the top of a peak, Kendall was startled to see over three dozen wild horses roaming the field; three were just colts, barely six months old. The cowboy slid off his horse and offered his hand. Staying quiet was understood. She joined the cowboy on the ground and smiled shyly as he squeezed her hand.

Another cowboy took the reigns of their horse, as the third cowboy handed over a fifty pound sack. Kendall tried to help carry the burlap bundle, but the cowboy she was with was bearing most of the weight. The two walked together closer and closer to the wild horses. They were being watched carefully by the head of the herd, a chestnut stallion whose ears twitched as they approached.

About fifteen feet from the youngest colt, the cowboy stopped. He tore open the sack and then lifted and carried it, releasing a trail of bright red apples onto the snow covered clearing. Kendall walked alongside the cowboy, as they kept their distance from the wild horses. A large black mare with a star on her forehead whinnied as she took in the scent of the ripe fruit.

A spotted black and white stallion was the first to approach. He stepped forward, bent his head, picked up an apple and began to eat. The others in the herd followed his lead.

The cowboy handed Kendall an apple, held onto her hand and guided it slowly toward the smallest colt. The small creature tentatively stepped forward and nibbled the fruit, all the while gazing up at her with large brown eyes. Kendall knew that she would never be able to fully explain how that moment touched her to her very core. The cowboy, cradling her hand, connected her to the world of the wild horses and re-opened her heart to the universe.

A minute passed silently and then the chestnut stallion lifted his head and ran off, which started a stampede deep into the woods. The cowboy helped Kendall back onto his horse and she relaxed back against his chest as they descended the mountain.

Kendall made it home safely early Christmas morning, her life forever changed. She caught one last glimpse as they rode off in a cloud of dust. Although some would refer to them as cowboy angels, to Kendall they were Christmas cowboys, the kind who ride out of the wilds of Montana.

~

MISTLETOE DINER

by Samantha Jaffe

The three girls tumble out of the concert, out of the big double doors that open into the freezing one a.m. air, out into the street buoyed by the crowd around them; hipsters who are hiding fur and vintage lace and ripped up tights behind knee length puffy snow coats because, after all, there are times when it is just too cold to be cool.

The girls, Emily, Shaun, and Christine, ride this surge of humanity down the street and around the corner and two blocks west to Moe's All-Night Diner, where the neon sign refracts off the snowflakes that are pooling on the sidewalk. Right now Moe's has its Christmas decorations up: fake holly and vinyl mistletoe.

Moe's is a real diner, a place where, if you show up often enough, the waitresses know your name and how you take your coffee and wonder at you when you come at a different time or day. But for these three girls this is their normal time: Friday night after a concert at the Paradise Rock Club, too many hours spent dancing and sweating and swaying and singing along to lyrics they all know by heart. The Paradise Rock Club was where John Mayer played in the 90's when he came to Boston, but now it's all about Kate Nash and The Expendables and Tokyo Police Club.

They sit down at their usual table, Emily and Shaun on one side and Christine on the other, next to the pile of artificial down that is dripping all over the red vinyl seat. Christine always sits with the coats, because that's how Christine is. Her brown bangs fall into her eyes and she orders an Oreo milkshake from Bea, their favorite waitress, even though it's 28 degrees outside and two weeks till Christmas. Emily and Shaun roll their eyes because sometimes Christine is just so incredibly Christine-ish. Emily has tea and Shaun has hot chocolate with a candy cane in it and the two of them split a piece of apple pie while Christine has rhubarb, of course Christine likes rhubarb, she likes it because it is the one that no one else likes.

The three of them met their freshman year, sometime during the second week of school. Emily says it was at a party and Shaun thinks it was outside their dorm and Christine honestly says she doesn't remember. The three of them couldn't be more different: Emily, from San Diego, all long legs and a camera constantly attached to her face. Shaun, blonde and pixie-like, a former dancer who loves 90's pop and metal, is pretentious about being from Manhattan, and only dates boys with long hair. Christine, whose big Italian family calls her constantly even though she only lives 20 minutes away now that she's at school. Somehow, through the course of freshman year and parties and dropping classes and acing classes and boyfriends (Christine) and not boyfriends (Shaun) and volleyball seasons (Emily) the three of them have forged a friendship that's real, none of this "first semester in college starter friends" stuff.

Emily and Shaun call Christine out when she's being difficult (which is often). Shaun and Christine make Emily forget about volleyball and just take the T somewhere random to get a little lost. And Emily and Christine yell at Shaun when she continuously denies the fact that she is in love with Peter, who is, incidentally, also in love with her. So sometime between the classes and concerts and coffee and study breaks and Sunday brunches and 1 am pie stops, the three of them have arrived here: Moe's Diner, 1:30 a.m. on December 15th, a very late Monday night or a very early Tuesday morning, with a week left until the end of their first semester of their sophomore year and 10 days until Christmas.

"Can I get you girls anything else?"

Emily looks up, confused. She was ready to ask Bea about her nephew who is sixteen and causing his whole family incredible distress as only sixteen year old boys can, and is arrested by this voice which is decidedly male, and decidedly not Bea. Instead it's a tall dark-haired boy in cool thrift store pants who is managing to make the apron tied around his waist look endearing.

"Um. I think we're okay," Emily stutters. Shaun looks at Christine pointedly. Christine asks for another milkshake, strawberry this time.

"Another milkshake?! That was your brilliant save?" Shaun whispers as cute waiter boy walks away.

"I know! I panicked! It's fine, at least this way Em and her complete and total lack of game will look really good in comparison," Christine laughs. Emily glares at both of them.

"Stop it! Just... cut it out! He's our

waiter, for gods sake!" she says, grey eyes glinting as she tries to be stern.

"Exactly," Shaun says. "This is perfect. He's cute, and he doesn't look like he plays lacrosse, so he won't remind you of Michael and you don't need to freak out. He'll fall in love with you as soon as you make eye contact with him like a normal person."

"I almost feel bad for the guy. He really has no hope," Christine muses, picking at her bright yellow painted nails.

"Shutup shutup shutup! You guys are the WORST I can't believe you—" Emily's rant is cut off by the return of the waiter with Christine's milkshake.

"I brought extra straws, no offense but you don't look big enough to finish two milkshakes on your own." He laughs down at Christine.

She smiles, " But I can try!" and then glares across the table at Emily. Emily glares back, then looks up at the waiter and smiles, shyly. Over the course of the last year and a half Shaun and Christine have learned that

Emily's smile has approximately the same effect on East Coast boys as a Yankees/Red Sox game: they're fascinated, mesmerized, and unable to look away. The cute waiter doesn't stand a chance.

"Uh. Do you guys need anything else?" he asks.

"You already asked us. We're great, though, thanks!" Shaun grins up at him.

"Right. Sorry! Um. Well let me know if you need anything." And the cute waiter bolts for the kitchen.

"Chris did you see that?! He was blushing!" Shaun is practically jumping out of her seat. "Seriously Em, you have a lethal weapon in that mouth of yours. We could bottle it and make millions. 'Cept we'd need to bottle your face too... I feel like it wouldn't be as effective without the whole classically beautiful thing."

"Stop! Please stop! Now I'm embarrassed and he's embarrassed and everyone is so, so embarrassed!" Emily is rattled. Her sun-streaked brown hair is falling out of its loose ponytail and into her face and she yanks her hair elastic out in frustration. The long waves flow past her shoulders and catch the light, just as the waiter walks by their table. Christine starts laughing.

"You could not have timed that better if you planned it. I swear, it's lucky you're clueless. The day your hormones kick in and catch up with the rest of you Shaun and I are just going to make ten tons of popcorn and follow you around while you lay waste to the male population. I've never been so excited."

Emily lets out a muted scream of frustration and flops her head onto the black and white checked table. Shaun finishes the last of Christine's strawberry milkshake, slurping loudly. Emily checks her phone, sees that it's 2:30 a.m.

"Okay. Waaaay past my bedtime. Let's go, taxi's on Mama. Luckily, she just sent me more 'shopping money'," Emily says.

"I just love it when your mother pays for taxis." Shaun licks the straw, getting every last drop of milkshake. All three of them get up and pay the check. When Christine goes back to the table to drop off the tip, she sees a napkin lying on the table with the words, "For the girl with the great smile: Alex – 617-555-9887 Merry Christmas."

"Guys, guys, guys!" She sprints outside, coat flying around her like a flag.

"Em. Check it out. He left you something." She's giggling, unable to contain herself. Shaun reads it and freaks out too. Even Emily, who never gets excited about boys, allows herself a thousand watt grin.

"He was pretty cute, huh?" She asks. The three of them stand under a flickering street lamp, waiting for a cab. The snowflakes swirl and spin, catching the light off the hoods of cars and the flash of Emily's camera. Their laughter rings out; they're laughing because it's almost Christmas and they're coming home from a concert and Christine ordered two milkshakes and Emily may have a date and Shaun looks like a fairy as she twirls in the snow and it's 2:30 in the morning on a Tuesday and they have class in 7 hours.

~

CHANGE OF HEART

by Vikram Kale

Los Angeles is a weird city. You can go from your apartment, to your car, to your office, back to your car in the evening, and then back to the apartment. You can live in this bubble your entire life and not connect with a single human being. I know this, because I had been living it for many years.

So, when my friend, Elizabeth egged me on to accompany her to the church on Christmas Eve, I agreed without much protest.

"Let's go worship a man-made idea of a man with a beard in the skies," I said sarcastically.

She just smiled it away; she was accustomed to me.

"I'm only going with you to enjoy the decorations," I said. "Other than that, religion is just a placebo for man's fear of existence."

She laughed at me with a what-the-heck-do-you-know, Mr. Atheist? look. We just liked each other's company; something just gelled. I had, despite my cynicism, visited this church on a few Sundays when life was just too much to handle. I'd admitted it to myself, but not to her.

As always, I was late to pick her up. We were late to the church.

Bright ambers lit up the brick layered building and arrays of tiny lights hugged its contours in a vivid display. As we parked in the lot, my eyes fell on the church sign: "My way IS the highway – God."

"No sarcasm tonight. It's Christmas." Liz said, reading my face.

The entrance was snowed up with

artificial frost to bring us into a wintery mood. I thought it was atypical of the ever-warm Los Angeles, but Liz felt it was a welcome contrast.

Reverend Woodall, the ever friendly, comforting pastor was giving his welcome speech as few of us rolled in. Fortunately, Liz and I had company so she couldn't give me that you-made-us-late-again look. The monochrome, warm light falling on the vivid stained glass windows was a mesmerizing sight.

Everyone, including the children, was festively dressed and lent their own to the conviviality. Liz fit right in; I think my lack of faith was just a tad bit too hard to conceal, but I was there to enjoy Liz's company anyways. Reverend Woodall introduced Roxanne, a church member who had lost her job that year.

"Who can say, 'I have kept my heart pure; I am clean and without sin?'" he quoted, and then explained how trying times were a part of our journey to wash away our sins and come closer to God.

"What a guilt trip," I quipped to Elizabeth.

"Keep it down," she replied.

Reverend Woodall then narrated how Roxanne had started her own small boutique with some help from family and friends and by that December had actually made more revenue than she would have on her job.

"Thus," the reverend continued, "the words of the Bible: 'For I know the plans I have for you… plans to prosper you and not to harm you, plans to give you hope and a future' are once again revealed to us."

"Oh! I see," I exclaimed. "Well, I would like to know His plans for --"

"Vijay," Liz interjected.

"What?"

"Shush."

At times, she wondered how I could be so irreligious, coming from India.

"Let us renew our hopes and our spirits and join each other in celebrating the birth of His only Son," Woodall concluded.

We stood up for the choir song. I struggled to find the right hymn in the book and missed singing the first stanza. I fumbled into the middle of the song and pretended singing. From the corner of my eye, I could see Liz giggling.

"What? At least I am trying," I chuckled.

A few eyebrows raised around us. We quickly joined them in finishing the last stanza, before taking our seats.

Reverend Nugent, grey-haired and genteel, came on stage and narrated a very personal story about how she once was disillusioned with her "boring and despair-filled life" in Ohio and through a miracle meeting had met her now husband, which changed her spirit forever. "His Grace had awakened me," she stated. "From then on, I was sure I was on the right path – the path of developing my relationship with God through repentance for my sins."

"Sins?" I blurted.

Elizabeth asked me to "keep it down."

"So what are your sins, then?" I asked her like a spoilt kid who wouldn't shut up.

"Later. Not now."

"Oh, so you haven't even done anything wrong, yet you --"

A violin string interrupted my stubborn mouth. Thankfully. The church band started playing. We all rose and sang the last hymn of the night. This time I did it right. After the introduction of some new members to the church, we all chorused the Lord's Prayer, my favorite part. I had committed it to memory the very first time I had read it in my life. I don't know how or why, but it always had a calming effect on me.

As the orchestra unfurled the last, and hypnotically beautiful composition of the night, the ushers moved gracefully down the aisles. I had always admired their poise, but never donated. "I am not supporting organized religion," I remarked to Elizabeth, as though she didn't know that already.

"It's to support the spirit of coming together," she explained.

"All religions are – "

She gestured an envelope to me. I turned around.

An usher was right behind me. I dropped the envelope into his basket and waited for him to go forward, then turned to Elizabeth.

"Suppressive." I finished my thought.

"Thanks for waiting," she said. "You and your atheistic rants."

"Well, to you I am an atheist, but to God, I am loyal opposition."

"What movie is that from? Stardust Memories?" she jested.

This was one of the disadvantages of being with Elizabeth. I couldn't hide my sources and impress her. We realized people were waiting for us to move. So, we got up and walked outside to the reception.

Poinsettias and brilliant, multi-color-ed lights cheered up the church lawn. An elaborate Santa Claus glided above us along with a "Merry Christmas" neon.

Amidst the festivities, we found a table and sat down with our hot coffee, which the wonderful, warm-hearted Ms. Coates had served us at the catering table. The evening was beautiful… until I spoke again.

"So, what is your sin? Did you kill someone?" I asked Elizabeth.

She rolled her eyes and said, "It's not supposed to be literal."

"No, c'mon. Tell me."

"You know about my accident when I was nine? I got hit by a car when I was bicycling."

"That's not your sin. That was the car driver's fault. "

"Yeah, but my life kind of has been falling apart since then."

"I think you're doing fine."

"Vijay, you know my parents split when I was eleven and how toxic that was for me!"

"I know, but that's not due to your sin or your fault."

"Yeah, but I have always wondered why bad things happen to me with such ferocity. Perhaps, I need to repent and ask for forgiveness from Him for anything

I may have done."

"I know. I understand how difficult and sad things have been at times, but it's not your fault. You didn't deserve all this."

"How do you know?"

"It's crystal clear. You haven't done anything bad to anyone. You're a fine young woman. And stuff happens in life – to anyone."

"You know how people say 'the glass is half empty'? For me, the glass is half empty and the rest of it is filled with poison."

Those words reverberated through me. I wanted my friend to see the truth and stop feeling guilty about her existence.

"You have not sinned, Elizabeth. The church and its manipulative ideology are all just a man made farce."

"How do you know?"

"How do I know? Because it's all imaginary."

"Life is too mysterious."

"Yeah, but guilt tripping won't help and it's not truthful. I want you to be happy."

"I'm happy coming here. So what's wrong?"

"What's wrong is that the pastor makes you feel guilty."

"Hopeful. The pastor makes me feel hopeful."

"But it's false hope."

"No, it's not."

"It is," I asserted.

"Not," she said, feeling cornered.

"How so? Tell me." I persisted, ready to show her the truth once and for all.

"Because despite all my past, I met you." she blurted out, and then looked away.

My eyes unblinking, my hands still. Every alphabet of that sentence coursed through my body and touched my being. I look at this friend I had known for years, but blinded! Suddenly, the blindfold was removed. Reverend Woodall's voice saying, "For I know the plans I have for you," rung in my ears louder than the traffic on the street. Life returned to my hands. My eyes blinked and took notice of the eagerness in Elizabeth's eyes. I smiled at her and held her hand assuredly. She smiled back at me.

Pin drop silence.

We could hear our hearts beat. Gently, I guided her to leave. Oblivious to the merriment, we trod lightly through the now ephemeral surroundings.

Usually I would just get into the driver's seat, but this time I opened her door first.

"I will be right back," I suddenly said.

"Where are you going?"

I hurried into the church. The room was empty. I scanned around, hoping to see the one person I wanted to see. Ah! The usher. I ran up to him. Pulled out my wallet, dropped every dollar and penny I had into his basket. He was amused. On my way out, I quickly turned around, looked at the Man on the Cross and bowed Namaste, my Indian way. The usher chuckled, but what did he expect from me? That's the best I could think of in that moment.

I sprinted back to the parking lot.

Her car door was still open; I took in the sight of Elizabeth waiting for me, adorned by the shimmering Christmas lights. I closed her door, and then got into the driver's seat.

"Where did you go?" she inquired curiously.

I started the car.

"Did you forget something inside?" she asked again.

"No. I just decided to support 'the Spirit of coming together.'"

As we drove out of the lot, my eyes fell on the church sign again: "My way IS the highway - God." Elizabeth scanned my face. This time, I smiled. She smiled with me.

~

MISSILE DEFENSE AND SANTA TRACKING

by Aldo Spadoni

For more than half a century, the North American Aerospace Defense Command (NORAD) has watched the skies, defending America against intruding bombers, missiles, and . . . Santa Claus! Every year on Christmas Eve since 1955, NORAD has tracked Santa's frenzied flight path as he rockets across the globe to deliver his presents. How did this curious state of affairs come about? As it turns out, it all started with a simple mistake.

Back in 1955, before there was a single human-made object in space, the world's only real astronaut was Santa Claus. But it was also the time of the Cold War and CONAD, America's Continental Air Defense Command, watched the skies. During that year, a Sears Roebuck store in the city of Colorado Springs had the wonderful idea of including a phone number in its advertising where children could call Santa Claus.

The ads were printed in the local newspaper and on Christmas Eve 1955, excited children placed their calls to Santa. But the phones began to ring at CONAD instead of the North Pole, because the telephone number had been misprinted!

USAF Colonel Harry Shoup was the man in charge at CONAD that night. One can only imagine what transpired when the first call came in.

"CONAD. Colonel Shoup here."

A tiny voice says, "Santa?"

"Excuse me??"

"Santa, this is Johnny. I'd like a G.I. Joe, a Slinky and maybe an Etch-a-Sketch."

"I beg your pardon??"

"Oh yeah, I need an Erector Set too!"

"Who is this??"

"It's Johnny, Santa, like I said."

Shoup is annoyed and barks, "Get off this line immediately! Do you realize I can have your parents thrown in jail for this kind of infraction?"

The boy is taken aback and starts to sob. "But Santa, I've been extra good this year!"

Shoup is furious at this point. "If you call me Santa one more time, I'll dispatch the Military Police to track you down and have you arrested as a juvenile delinquent!"

"Please Santa, don't give me a lump of coal! I need Silly Putty at least!"

After the initial confusion and a few more calls, it dawned on Colonel Shoup and the CONAD staff that these were not the Soviets calling, masquerading as America kids intent on causing mayhem. Colonel Shoup did not issue orders to have these kids arrested or launch a counterstrike. Instead, once he realized what was happening, the Colonel mellowed and told his staff to provide Santa's current location as best they could to all children that called. Whether or not they ever sent a bill to Sears for their services is unknown, but what is known is that the Santa Tracking tradition was born.

In 1958, the United States joined forces with Canada, CONAD became NORAD and the Christmas Eve tracking of Santa persisted. An ever-increasing army of volunteers continued to provide this critical information in several languages to inquiring children around the world. In 1997 the Santa Tracking System got its own website, greatly expanding the ability to keep up with demand and making the task much more manageable for the volunteers.

The Santa Tracking System has kept pace with the information age and kids of all ages can now track Santa's whereabouts through Facebook, Twitter, YouTube, Flickr, and http://www.facebook.com/l/a8d0bPjVjtijg-FTsN3YrGOdjLg;TroopTube.tv and also Norad has its own website for tracking at http://www.noradsanta.org.

Those who might have concern about the use of taxpayer dollars can rest assured that this is a volunteer effort conducted with creativity and imagination, with little impact on NORAD's operations. Santa continues his tradition of cooperation with NORAD as well as other defense agencies across the planet. In this way, he can get on with his business and avoid any unpleasant "mystery missile" incidents.

Every year, as part of the agreement, NORAD will tell you where Santa is and where he's going, but the true performance capabilities of Santa's sleigh remains a closely guarded secret.

Merry Christmas to all and to Santa, a good flight!

~

MY CHRISTMAS ANGEL

A True Story

By Michael Habte

I was living in Dallas for fifteen years, was completely burnt out with my job. I was also grieving. My brother-in-law, who was my best friend, had passed away. I think I was going through a mid-life crisis, and it didn't help that I was working fifty hours a week as a waiter and assistant manager at a very fine restaurant. I was exhausted mentally, physically and emotionally. It was very difficult for me to handle all these problems by myself and I had the worst Thanksgiving of my life. So, I made a decision to take a short vacation and leave town without giving notice.

It had been extremely cold in Texas, so I chose to go to warm and sunny Los Angeles. At the Dallas airport I found myself in the midst of the holiday season and I promised myself that I would relax, enjoy and have fun, but on the plane I got caught up with the holiday blues. I didn't know anyone in L.A., but I took a leap of faith and started talking to God to give me strength. I prayed hard on the way to California.

When I arrived in Los Angeles, I rented a hotel room. My favorite places to hang out were around the beaches of Venice and Santa Monica. The ocean and the landscape were calming, but I still felt like I was on an emotional rollercoaster. Sometimes I would ask myself why am I here. I could not get a clear answer. Even though I am a people person, I felt lonely.

This was my spiritual journey, soul searching with God. I prayed and meditated often, which uplifted me a little. I began to develop a strong belief in God and also I started to believe in myself. I told myself that all these problems will pass. At times, I was doubtful, but my resistance and belief became stronger. I did not want to give up. I told myself that there was a light at the end of the tunnel. These were really difficult times, but the spiritual strength I developed eased my pain. It was too much to handle, but by the grace of God, it was bearable.

On the morning of Christmas Eve, it was a nice day. I decided to go to Venice Beach to relax. I called a taxi to take me there and started a conversation with the driver. He was my countryman, another East African. He asked me what brought me here from Dallas. I replied, "Vacation." Throughout the conversation, he asked me if I had plans for Christmas. I answered that I did not. I just wanted to be alone.

I think the driver felt badly for me, so he cordially invited me to come to his house on Christmas Day to have lunch with his family. It was a kind offer, but I declined the invitation. I was not in the mood for a celebration. The driver persisted, but still my answer was no thank you. Finally, I arrived at the beach. I thanked the driver and paid my fare. As I was about to leave, he handed me a slip of paper with his telephone number and address and said, "In case you change your mind." I put the piece of paper in my pocket and went on my way thinking, "Why is this guy so insistent?"

The next morning, it was Christmas Day. I woke up refreshed, a little upbeat, but bored. I decided to stay in and watch television. By noon, I was hungry. As I was dressing, I found the piece of paper that the taxi driver had given me. All of a sudden, I decided to have lunch at the taxi driver's house. I was suddenly craving a holiday meal. I took a taxi to the address he had given me. My fellow countryman opened the door and welcomed me to his home with a smile and said, "You changed your mind." He offered me something to drink. I requested a beer and sat on the couch. I opened the bottle and took a sip, when someone knocked on the front door.

When the door opened, a very beautiful, elegant woman stepped inside the entryway and spoke quietly to the taxi driver. I looked at the young woman again and again. I could not believe my eyes. Her presence was so strong, her beauty was sparkling and her personality was dazzling. Still, I could not believe my own eyes because I knew this woman long ago when we were both in high school in Asmara, Eritrea.

I was overwhelmed and blown away. How could this happen? Ten thousand miles away, after twenty five years and now in Los Angeles, to come across this woman I knew from my past… I was frozen.

I could not find words to explain or express my feelings. I was so overwhelmed. I was asking myself if I were crazy or if this were a dream. Emotions were flowing through my entire body.

I was sweating, my lips sealed. I could

not say a word. She stayed only a few minutes, dropped off a Christmas gift and left.

I was still in shock after she had gone. I could not eat or drink. My host was concerned and asked me what was wrong, "Are you sick or not feeling well?" I answered that I was fine.

After I gathered myself, I started speaking just a little. I asked the lady of the house, "Is the woman who dropped by a good friend of yours?" She smiled and nodded. I explained that I knew her long ago and I requested her telephone number. The host and his wife exchanged a look of concern. The wife said she could not give me her phone number, as I was a stranger. She asked why didn't I speak to the woman when she there. My host and his wife were right. They didn't know me and they didn't know that I had been overwhelmed with emotion, unable to speak. Normally, I am a very brave man and can ask a woman for her phone number, but at the time, for some reason, I was very weak.

I decided not to go back to Dallas, but instead to pursue this beautiful angel. She was my true love; God had sent her as a Christmas gift.

It took me three months just to search out her telephone number. I called and was so happy and relieved to speak with her. Her voice was sweet. She was someone I had liked since high school and my feelings had only gotten stronger.

We began seeing each other. I started to open up and express my love for her and she would ask if I were crazy. My answer was yes, I am crazy about you. Sometimes she was doubtful, but gradually as we spent time together, she trusted my feelings for her and soon they were reciprocated. As time went by, we became soul mates. Our views of the world and our outlook on life were the same. Sometimes, before I started to say something, she would say it. We were compatible. We were meant for each other.

It was a true miracle on Christmas Day.

After dating for three months, I proposed and she said yes. I arranged for us to marry in a hotel by the ocean in beautiful Manhattan Beach. I wanted to do something special for my bride, so I rented a vintage 1957 white Thunderbird convertible two-seater and we cruised along the ocean and around the streets of Hollywood.

When we came to the corner of Fairfax and Olympic Boulevard my wife looked up and called out in surprise. She saw the billboard I had specially rented for our wedding day, it was printed with my wife's name and "I love you with all my heart." My wife laughed and hugged me tightly, as we drove back and forth past the billboard that announced my declaration of love. My wife is one in a billion. She is everything to me, a wonderful package, perfect, sweet, calm, kind and pure.

It has been twelve years now and to this day, our love is still growing. We are blessed to have a beautiful daughter.

I am very grateful that God gave me a pure, true love on Christmas Day.

~

SNOWBIRD

by Valerie Scott

Although she was old enough to know better, ten-year-old Willow Rowe wished she had a magic sleigh so she could run away. She was lonely and scared and missed her best friend, Amanda. All she wanted for Christmas was to be in a place where somebody remembered her face.

Almost a year ago, she and her father, Matthew had moved from Long Beach, California to Snowflake, Arizona. He had taken a job at the Apache Railway Company which employed most of the town of five thousand. Though it rarely snowed in

Snowflake, the town held its annual Snow Festival the week before Christmas.

Willow's fourth grade classmates were looking forward to the task of making snow-themed costumes and competing for "best in snow." Willow wasn't that excited. Each child was to wear a homemade costume and was expected to sing or tell a story about what made them glow like snow. By applause, the winners, a boy and a girl, would receive a snow globe which contained intricately crafted, miniature statues of the town's founders, Erastus Snow and William Flake, dressed as snowmen standing before the first house built in Snowflake in 1878.

The festival culminated in the crowning of the high school Snowflake King and Queen. Once chosen, the King and Queen judged the annual snow-cake bake-off. Fruitcake, cupcakes, cheesecake and angel food cake could be entered and then eaten by all. Most of the women in the town entered and even several men who fancied they were chefs. The kids' favorite competition was the best snowman contest. A snow machine provided the snow for that one and only day there had to be snow in Snowflake.

It was the day before the annual festival and Willow came home greeted by the ever- present Skye Blossom, who was busy decking the halls. "Have you decided what you're going to be for this year's show?"

How did she know about her part in the show? She didn't have any kids. Skye must be a spy.

"I thought I'd be a snow-fro and dance like Beyoncé and sing 'I can feel your halo, halo, halo…',," Willow was moving provocatively until Skye said, "you'll never get to heaven if you carry on like that."

"I thought your people believed in the happy hunting ground," Willow said with smirk. "Can you at least make it rain?"

"I'm afraid my powers have dissipated over time. Now it's homework for you and cooking for me. I'm working on a special recipe for the snow bake," Skye said.

"What kind of cake?"

"A Navajo snow cake. And yes, it has special powers," Skye said. "If you finish all your homework, I'll let you sample the magic." Skye gently brushed over Willow's shoulder. "I think you were born to play a snowbird. Its spirit suits you. The real name is Junco and it has dark eyes and comes in various colors. It's a beautiful little bird, just like you."

"If I were a bird, I'd fly back to California. Dad seems to like it here…and you." She shrugged her shoulders, "I miss my friends."

"Sometimes you are in the right place at the right time and you don't even know it."

"Is that some kind of Indian voodoo thing?"

"I think Whoopi said it on 'The View'," Skye laughed, bent down and kissed Willow on the top of her head. "Now go."

Matthew Rowe had hired Skye when they first moved to Snowflake. She was the housekeeper and Willow-watcher while he was at work. She was part Navajo and part something else. Skye was born and raised in Snowflake. Her brothers and sisters left as soon as they could and her parents stayed until they passed away. Skye loved the town and had no desire to leave. She started babysitting when she was a teenager, realizing she was good with children and thought that one day she would go to college to become a teacher. The years went by and Skye found herself cooking and cleaning for family after family, yet somehow never having one to call her own.

Skye was the most beautiful woman Willow had ever seen. Her eyes were as green as grass and her long hair flowed like autumn leaves. Willow's own hair stuck to her head like a Brillo pad and even though she was almost eleven, she looked years younger. Her tiny caramel colored frame and wild hair made her stand out. One day, Skye offered to braid her hair. When she was done, Willow had a headache, but didn't have the heart to tell Skye, because she was so pleased by her handy work. Willow had never had cornrows and when she looked in the mirror, she liked what she saw.

Willow entered the kitchen and her nose was hit by delight. She rushed over to the kitchen island and watched as Skye pulled out two cake pans from the oven. "That smells awesome," Willow said as she was about to poke a hole in one. Skye stopped her and said, "Good things come to those who wait." From the oven, Skye pulled out a smaller cake pan. "You can have your very own magic cake after dinner."

Willow felt love for Skye. She didn't remember if she had ever called her mother, mom. Her father told her that she was in heaven. Willow wished Skye was her mother.

At six o'clock her father came home and the three shared a wonderful pot roast. "So when are we going to start turning me into a bird?" Willow inquired.

"Don't you want to have some cake first?" Skye asked. "Not right now, I want to get started on my wings. Can I be excused, Dad?"

Matthew nodded yes and asked Skye, "What is she up to?"

Clearing the table she said, "I think your little girl is getting ready to fly the coop. I found a half-packed suitcase under her bed."

"I'll talk to her," Matthew said. Skye gently held his hand and said, "Why don't I talk to her first?"

Matthew pulled her closer. She lovingly pushed him back. "If she finds out about us, it might make matters worse."

Willow returned to the kitchen just in time to hear what Skye had said. She had noticed her father was different since Skye came into their lives.

At first she thought he was just relieved to have someone to help around the house, but she was beginning to think there were something more. Willow rushed back to her room before they noticed her. She pushed her half-packed suitcase further under her bed.

The next day the competition was ice

cold during her fourth grade judging for "the best in snow." Willow was up against, a snowflake, a snow cone, a flake cake and a snow cap. Skye had really out done herself on the costume. Willow actually thought she could fly, if she tried. It was now her turn to take center stage. She spread her wings and stepped up to the microphone and read a poem she had written with a little help from Skye.

See the pretty snowbirds flying
  in the Skye;
On the tree and on the rooftops,
  soft and light they fly
Covered by the snowflakes,
  not a wing to be seen
All look soft and white, but you'll
  notice their many colors
  when they take flight

Willow received a standing ovation and won the snow globe. Inside the globe, Willow swore Misters Snow and Flake were applauding her as well. Willow looked up, right at Skye and mouthed, thank you. When she looked at her father, he was wiping a few tears from his eyes. He smiled at Willow and mouthed I love you, baby. Willow had never seen her father cry. She found herself fighting back her own tears. She loved her father more than anything at that moment. Minutes later another announcement was made. Skye's snow cake had won first prize, a gold plated spatula trophy. When the three of them arrived home, they feasted on another of Skye's cakes and drank hot chocolate with marshmallows on top.

Matthew had Skye join them for Christmas morning and Willow loved opening up her presents. Then her father said, "I have something to ask both of you." He took Willow and Skye by the hand and led them to the fireplace.

Matthew reached in his robe pocket and pulled out a velvet box, bent down on one knee, and opened the box, reveling a stunning diamond and turquoise ring.

He put it on Skye's finger. He reached in his other pocket and pulled out another velvet box and handed it to Willow. She opened it and pulled out a shiny gold locket.

"Willow, you will always have my heart, but with your blessing, I'd like to share our hearts and our lives with Skye. I asked her last night if she would marry me and she said she would marry us."

"Does this mean I get to call you mom?" she asked Skye tentatively.

Skye hugged Willow and said, "I'd be honored." Skye looked up and saw a snowbird perched on the window sill. The bird spread its tiny wings and flew away.

~

CHRISTMAS IN KENYA

by Charles Kamuyu

Christmas commemorates the birth of Jesus Christ and nearly every Christian celebrates it. Yet, the holiday season, regardless of one's religion, is also a time to focus on what's important. The holidays give families the opportunity to draw close together. In Africa, people usually travel from the cities into the countryside ("upcountry") to be with their families.

Christmas in Kenya is a joyous time. All the children look forward to their Christmas presents, which usually include a new outfit, with a matching pair of shoes.

Special holiday food is prepared; "chapatti" (African bread), "rice pilau, stews and riyo" (mashed potatoes, peas and corn) and of course "nyama choma" (barbeque). And just as the turkey is for Thanksgiving, in Africa, the goat is essential for Christmas. The father of the family will have specially raised and tended to the goat throughout the year, and it will be respectfully slaughtered for the meal.

During the day and into the night, there is much singing, dancing, riddle and story telling. Each tale is filled with satire, various themes and a great deal of lessons for all ages. These stories and riddles are usually told by the grandparents, and one must keenly listen and learn, as most of the stories have not been written down. One such story, "The Bat", is my personal favorite. The story illustrates the dangers of a person who betrays a common cause.

* * * * *

There was once a drought in the Jungle where many animals lived. The grass and the rivers dried up. All the animals, particularly the hoofed-ones and those that don't fly, faced great starvation and thirst. The animals that didn't fly became extremely desperate and knew they faced imminent death. The winged-creatures did not experience such severe problems, as they could fly and look for food and water elsewhere.

The non-fliers called a meeting to figure out what they could do to stay alive. The meeting was also attended by the winged-ones. When the time came to choose a leader, the winged-ones said that they were also entitled to choose their own leaders. The chairman's seat went to the Eagle and the Ostrich became the vice chairman. The animals without wings had their own election and chose the Elephant to lead them, with the Lion as the assistant. The Elephant rose to speak and declared that he had spotted a well that contained a small amount of water. It was suggested that all the animals should gather together and head to the well. The plan was for them to work together and to stamp their feet on the damp area around the well, thereby producing more water.

The leader of the flying creatures declared, "We the winged-ones don't have the problems that those who cannot fly have. We can, and do fly to where we are able to get water. Therefore, we, the winged-ones, should not concern ourselves with the mission that has been suggested."

The Lion was very offended by the Eagle's speech and asked whether in the event of water being provided, would the winged-creatures be allowed to drink it. The hoofed-animals cried out, "No!" They further conferred and announced,

"If we dig for water and find it, we shall fight you winged-ones, if you dare to drink it."

The Eagle declared, "Let's fly off, as the meeting is over." All the winged creatures flew off, but the Ostrich, who had wings but could not fly.

The Ostrich chose instead to sprint towards the promised well. It should be noted that it is said that the Ostrich acquired its capacity to speed from that very day.

It was chaos for the non-winged animals. Those that could not fly were burdened by a number of things; one of them being that they were blowing up too much dust when they were running, so they were not able to get to their destination quickly. They however did get there, and they stomped and dug near the well, causing the water to swell.

The winged-ones stealthily arrived and began to steal the water. Soon their thievery was discovered. The non-fliers then appointed the Rabbit and the Squirrel to guard the well. These two animals were chosen because they were known for being crafty, but still, the winged-creatures still managed to steal water.

The non-fliers decided they had no choice but to go to war against the winged-animals. One day before reckoning, the winged-animals had the Bat come before them to declare which side he was on. There seemed to be some ambivalence on his part.

The Eagle said to the Bat, "We are sure you are on our side, because you have wings and can fly just like us."

The Bat replied, "Just have another look at me and you will see that my wings are not feathered like yours. Then look at my head and you will realize that I have no beak, but instead I have a mouth and teeth, while none of you have that." The Bat continued, "Haven't you noticed that I don't lay eggs like you, but instead I give birth like the hoofed-animals?" He cleared his throat and declared to the winged-animals, "For these reasons I won't join the battle on your side."

The Bat flew off after he had his say. When the hoofed-animals learned about his deflection from the winged-creatures, they celebrated and invited the Bat to join their ranks in the forthcoming battle.

The animals were surprised by the Bat's response. "What are you talking about?" the Bat replied. "Have another look at me and tell me how I look. Who of you has wings? If you look at me closely, you will see that my legs don't have hooves like yours. I have claws and although I give birth like you, I don't belong to your clan." The Bat flew off after he had his say to the non-fliers.

War was waged the very next day and victory started going the way of the hoofed-creatures.

The winged-animals conceded defeat and offered to finish the necessary work on the well. The hoofed-ones agreed to the terms of the settlement and a peace agreement was forged.

Soon after, a reconciliation meeting was called. When the talks were in session, the issue of the Bat was discussed. The question was, "To which side does the Bat belong to?" Each camp recounted what the Bat had said on the eve of the battle.

When the whole truth was revealed, the gathered animals unanimously agreed to expel the Bat from their fraternity. The winged-animals warned it to never again fly in the air, while the flightless-ones banned the Bat from walking on the ground.

The assembly then unanimously cursed the Bat to forever sleep upside down.

To this very day the Bat is still stung by this curse. That is why the Bat moves at the speed of lightening at night, for fear of being spotted by the other animals. The curse also explains why the Bat clutches the branches of a tree with its claws, sleeping with its head facing down.

* * * * *

The story of the Bat illustrates the dangers of sitting on the fence when the community is making an important group decision. It calls for individuals to join in and get involved in charting a common destiny towards progress. Such stories are told at Christmas to unify people and to safeguard against division and isolation.

Christmas in Kenya is widely celebrated, not because of its religious connection, but more so because it brings people together. Every Christmas is always different from the previous one. There will be additions to the family, marriages and more children.

As time passes, when grandparents are gone, their stories, riddles and compassion are the great memories that are left with us. No one can survive without friends and family. They bring us joy and love. When needed, they give us a sympathetic ear or a shoulder to cry on. They offer helpful advice and are with us to share in our laughter and our tears. This Christmas, my wife Joyce, our two children and I will be upcountry in Kenya, celebrating Christmas with our family and friends. We say to you: Kuwa Na Krismasi Njema ("We Wish You a Merry Christmas").

~

TRIPLETS

by Howard Steinberg

"**B**oys, stop fidgeting. You'll spill the hot chocolate. I want you to pay attention to the story I'm going to tell you. I think you're old enough to understand. What are you now, nine, ten, and eleven?"

"Nine, ten, and eleven and a half, Grandpa," the oldest boy said while carefully adding another log to the fire in the fireplace.

Grandpa started his story. "A number of years ago, long before the three of you were born, Grandma and I had some friends named Albert and Bernice. They had three boys just like your mom and dad did, except the boys were triplets. Albert and Bernice named them Charles, Donald, and Eric. Grandma and I accused them of alphabetizing their family."

The two older boys laughed, and then they explained what was funny to their younger brother. He giggled.

"C, D, and E were healthy little guys.

I remember them jabbering away at each other. Unfortunately, the triplets were orphaned. With no family members able to adopt the boys, the county adoption agency tried to find a single home for the triplets. With no success, the authorities decided the value of the love of a new mother and father outweighed the value of the togetherness of blood brothers. So, the triplets were to be separated—forever.

"Charles was adopted first. He was raised, along with his new sister, in a household with a fervent belief in the Democratic Party and all the good things that stemmed from their liberalism."

Grandpa stopped and looked at each

of the youngsters. "You boys know what I'm saying?"

"Grandpa, we watch the news," the nine-year-old said.

Satisfied they understood what he was talking about, Grandpa went on. "Somehow, unexpectedly, that set of values of Charles' new family didn't include a belief in global warming." Again, Grandfather paused and looked around.

"Graandpaa," the ten-year old said.

"OK, you boys are with it. As you might expect, Charles accepted his parents' values as his values.

"Donald's new household had a different view of the world. His new mom, dad, and brother were proud to be Republicans. They were steeped in conservatism. They thought global warming was a joke, and Donald found no reason to question this set of beliefs.

"The third triplet, Eric, inherited a mom and dad without any other children. They were totally without allegiance to any political party but almost paranoid on the dangers of global warming. Eric became an expert on climate change, but after his eighteenth birthday, he never got around to register to vote.

"When they were eighteen, C, D, and E went off to college. And, by some strange coincidence of life—as happens in many movies—C and D ended up at the same college. Then, as if guided by some external force, or screenwriter, the two boys were paired as dorm roommates."

This time, all three of his grandchildren giggled, which pleased Grandpa.

"Try as they did, C and D could not control arguing daily on the virtue or disaster of pending legislation in Congress. It was inconceivable to Charles that Donald did not see the illogic of his position, and vice versa. It was only the basic good sense that had been instilled in both boys by their foster parents that kept them from physically punishing each other. However, antipathy was growing. In one last attempt to preserve some semblance of a relationship, they decided to go together to the annual, between-holidays, freshman party hosted by the three local colleges.

"Randomly seated at 'their' party table were three young women, one from each college, and another guy, Eric something or other was his name. It was noisy. The conversation led to a discussion of climate change and soon became heated. Charles and Donald, in a rare moment of complete agreement, ganged up on Eric, whose global warming arguments were persuasive and difficult to counter. After several back-and-forths, accusations took over, and the women left the table.

"Eric stood, clenched his fists, and said, 'If you morons weren't rich spoiled brats, you would see where you were leading the world.'

"Charles stood and said, 'If you were in an orphanage until you were five years old, you'd know what the real world was like.'

"Donald stood and said, 'I was adopted.'

"Eric lowered his head and looked over

his glasses at his adversaries. 'I too was an orphan.

I found out my birth name is Goodrow.'

"Charles and Donald, as if one, said, 'That's my birth name.'

"C, D, and E, with tears in their eyes, realizing they were brothers, moved around the table and into a three-way hug."

Grandpa was pleased with how intently his grandchildren had listened to his story. He ended with, "And so my good children, there are forces more powerful than the happenstance of left or right, or hot or cold."

~

CHRISTMAS TWISTER

by Dianna Brown

It was a small town in Indiana, a perfect time and place to have a flat tire. Ted Johnson smiled as he stepped from the car, removed his suit jacket, and tossed it in the back seat. "Don't eat that," he told the Old English sheepdog puppy, curled in up a small ball on the back seat.

"Oh Gunther wouldn't do that, would you?" Becky said. The eight week old puppy lifted his head in innocence, and Becky couldn't resist picking him up.

"Gunther?" Ted looked puzzled at his wife. "What kind of name is that?"

"Dignified. It's what our granddaughter told Santa his name would be."

"Always knew she was a bright girl." Ted chuckled. "Takes after her..."

"Grandmother." Becky interrupted playfully.

"All my girls are as smart as they are beautiful." Ted said with a chuckle. "But stubborn," he muttered as he headed to the trunk of the Lincoln which had seen better days.

"I heard that," Becky smiled. "Come on, Gunther, let's take a walk while Grandpa takes his foot out of his mouth." Ted called after her, "After twenty five years of marriage, two children and a grand-daughter, I've learned to love sole food." Ted lifted the spare tire and set to work replacing the flat one. Becky walked into the now harvested cornfield and set down the puppy.

With the corn crop gone she could see the rooftop of her childhood home. The old farm house still stood proudly on the hill.

As the crow flies, they were less then a mile away, but to drive there, it was nearly two miles. She turned to her husband.

"Ted, you're smiling." His wife scolded teasingly. "One would think you planned this flat tire."

Ted cleared his throat and quickly pasted a frown on his face. "Now why would that be? A flat tire is a very serious event."

"It is that." Becky, grinned, as she strolled back to the car. She enjoyed an unhurried moment with her husband and watched as the puppy pounced and attacked some remaining corn stubble.

"Well" she sighed, "It's Christmas Eve and we can't be too late. I should be there to help set up for dinner."

"It would be unforgivable to be late. Your mom has slaved away all week to decorate and fix an exquisite meal for everyone," Ted said removing the hub cap. "Dang it!" He gritted his teeth as the wrench slipped off the lug nut and he scraped his knuckles.

"Are you alright?" Becky asked.

"It's just a scratch," Ted said, "Add a new wrench to the Santa list. This one's rusty."

"Ted, you haven't been yourself these past few days. What's bothering you?"

Ted wrapped his handkerchief about his knuckles. "I'm just tired is all. It's the same thing every year, after year, after year."

"That's why it's called a tradition." Becky added as she lifted her face to the sun, enjoying the unusually warm weather.

"Your Aunt Sally having us all sing, 'The Twelve Days of Christmas'? When did that become a tradition?" Ted grimaced. "Or your cousin Betty's rock hard biscuits?"

"Well at least this year you, Jack and Dad won't be able to use them as hockey pucks," Becky teased. "The pond hasn't frozen yet."

Ted grinned sheepishly, removed the flat and rolled it aside, then placed the new tire on the wheel bolts. "How did you know about our little hockey game?"

"We all knew," Becky replied.

She frowned as she watched a large area of dark clouds roll in. "Ted we need to leave. The weather's changing and I don't like it." Becky looked around for the puppy, but he was gone. "Gunther?" Becky called out, as a loud crack of thunder split the air.

"Merciful Heaven, where did that come from?!" Ted exclaimed. Becky spotted Gunther heading deeper into the cornfield. "Ted, we have to hurry!" Becky shouted as she started up the hill. One of her high heels dug into the dirt and she fell. Ted rushed toward her.

Becky grimaced in pain, "I twisted my ankle. Please get the puppy. Oh! No!" She pointed to the clouds, "A tornado is forming!"

Ted reached out his hand, pulled his wife to her feet, "Let me get you to the car."

"No time, just get Gunther. I'll be fine." She started hobbling toward the car. The wind began to roar.

"This storm came out of nowhere," Ted gasped, as the dark spiraling mass of wind and debris hurled toward them. The tornado was now on the ground. Ted sprinted across the field, as a gust of wind knocked the little puppy off his feet.

With a dive Ted caught the puppy, held him tight and made a dash for the car, dodging a storm of dirt, tree limbs and corn stubble, being blown about in the wind. In one fluid movement, Ted opened the car door, tossed the pup to Becky who was already inside, got in and started the engine.

The engine roared to life and Ted pumped the gas pedal. The back tire spun, the car jack tipped and the car bumped forward. "I hope that tire holds. I only managed to get three of the five lug nuts on and they're not tightened down."

The tornado was just on the other side of a cropping of maple trees. The devil wind ripped a path through the trees as if they were tiny toothpicks. The thunderous roar grew in intensity.

"Where's your mom's storm shelter?" Ted asked.

"On the west side of the house," Becky instructed. Her eyes were full of fright as she looked out the rear window. She screamed over the roar of the wind, "We don't have twisters this time of the year!"

"A Christmas twister?:" Ted snapped with disbelief. "It's unheard of."

The tornado was catching up to them. The farmhouse driveway was now close by. Ted wrenched the steering wheel, making a hard right. The tires screeched and the car fishtailed. The spare tire wobbled, "Hold on, hold on." He willed the spare to stay in place. He accelerated up the driveway; it was lined on both sides with plastic candy canes and Christmas lights.

Further up the drive, Ted and Becky could see the family running in panic towards the storm shelter. Their son Jack, dressed in his Air Force uniform, was carrying his five-year-old daughter, Amanda.

"Jack is home! Why didn't you tell me our son was coming home?"

"He wanted to surprise you."

"Drive across the lawn," Becky pointed to where her father, was holding the storm shelter doors open. "Ted hurry," Becky screamed as Ted pumped the gas pedal.

"Hold on" he ordered and the car lurched forward.

They plowed through the Christmas decorations, sending them flying in all directions. The old Lincoln bumped and bounced over the rolling lawn, strings of red and white lights twisted around them.

Becky's father, Luke, saw them coming and renewed his struggle against the wind to keep the shelter door open. He motioned for them to hurry. Ted slammed on the brakes, brought the car to a skidding halt. "Go," he ordered, as Becky limped from the car, clutching the puppy tightly.

"Hurry, Ted." She called and looked over her shoulder.

Ted opened his car door only to feel the Lincoln lift off the ground. Becky screamed. Luke grabbed his daughter and forced her inside the shelter, then dashed in behind her, just as the car was swept away, carrying Ted with it.

Inside the storm shelter, Becky's mother took the puppy and her father held onto her, preventing Becky from running back outside into the storm. "Dad, please let me go. I need to get to Ted."

"We've gotta wait it out," Luke told his daughter.

The roaring wind, the pelting of hail and the flying debris only increased Becky's despair. Then, as quickly as it began, it ended. Everything was deadly silent. All in the shelter held their breaths waiting. Soon the warning sirens blasted the all clear signal. Becky dashed up the steps and out the doors.

The path of the freak tornado was plain to see. The debris field was filled. Becky could see the neighbor's barn had taken some damage and her parents' grain silo was gone. Her father came up and put his arms around her. "We'll go together and look for Ted" They headed down through the debris field.

Jack had gotten his car and drove up to them. "Mom, c'mon, we'll find him." They searched through fields and around fallen trees, avoiding power lines. When they finally arrived in town they drove up to the civic center. Police cars and fire trucks were parked in the street and even on the courthouse lawn.

Then Becky saw their car, wrapped around the base of a large tree. "There's the Lincoln!" Becky cried. It was insane. Becky's mind screamed, why were they laughing? Her husband was trapped in the car that had clearly smashed into a tree. "Ted!" Becky yelled, as she pushed her way through the crowd.

"Up here, honey" Ted called down to her. Her husband was trapped at the very top of the tree.

Becky gasped, seeing her husband wedged between two sturdy branches, wearing only a smile, one sock and a shoe. "Are you alright?" his wife called out.

"I'm fine, except for my modesty,"

he grinned. "Hey son, welcome home. How was your flight?"

"Not as wild as yours it seems," Jack chided. "They won't let us fly naked."

The firefighter ascended in the fire bucket and reached Ted, handing him a blanket. In minutes the firefighter had Ted safely back on the ground.

"I was so scared." Becky murmured as she pulled a few twigs out of his wind whipped hair.

"Me too," he whispered and they hugged.

Back at the farm house, Ted was now showered and dressed in a spare plaid shirt and jeans two sizes too large. He was seated at the dinner table next to his wife. Their granddaughter, Amanda, sat cradling her new puppy, Gunther.

As Ted heartily ate one of Cousin Betty's hard biscuits, Aunt Sally began her annual singing of "The Twelve Days of Christmas." Ted was quite pleased that he had drawn the twelfth day for his part to sing. As he waited his turn, he looked around the table he realized he no longer felt tired. He had rediscovered the joy of life and his family's odd traditions. When it was his verse to sing, he sang out loudly and off-key. The room filled with good natured laughter.

~

SECRET SANTA

by Lars Daniel Eriksson

Bobby was only five years old, so he knew that Santa Claus was real. Santa Claus lived in the North Pole, with his wife and all of the elves, of course. Everyone knew that.

Once a year Santa came to visit all of the houses of all of the good children and bring them presents. Bobby thought Santa must be a great man.

Bobby's older sister, Betty, was talking about Christmas for weeks, which felt like forever to Bobby. Betty was eight and a half, but she liked to say she was "almost nine." Betty annoyed Bobby, and Bobby did his best to annoy her. But because it was the holiday season, everyone was supposed to behave. That's what Mommy and Daddy said.

So while the rest of his family was watching a movie in the other room, Bobby took a peek into the closet in his parents' bedroom. He liked to try on his Daddy's shoes, which felt enormous; and he also enjoyed putting on his Daddy's coats, which were plush and felt like funny blankets.

On this night, just two days before Christmas, Bobby saw something he'd never seen before: Santa's clothes, all bundled together in his Daddy's closet.

Why did Daddy have Santa's clothes? How strange, Bobby thought, and reached out carefully to touch them -- then stopped.

Bobby checked his little hands to see that they were clean. They weren't, so he washed them in his parents' bathroom. He remembered his Mommy getting mad when he touched the furniture with dirty hands. Bobby liked being a good boy and he hoped it would be okay if he touched Santa's clothes now that his hands were super clean.

Maybe his Daddy knew Santa personally, and was saving the bundle of clothes to help Santa. This could be Bobby's only chance to touch Santa's clothes. It was like touching the cape of Superman!

Ever so cautiously, Bobby reached out and felt the soft red cloth, and then discovered Santa's red and white hat. Bobby gingerly picked it up and ran his fingers along the white cotton trim. Bobby put the large hat upon his head and laughed. One of two fluffy white balls on the end hit him gently on the nose and then rested beside his cheek, next to his ear. What would Santa say if he could see the look on Bobby's face? Smiling a grin so wide that he was beaming with joy, Bobby felt happy as a clam, when in walked his Daddy. His Daddy stopped in his tracks and looked at his boy.

"You shouldn't be snooping in there," his Daddy said, smiling just the same.

"I wasn't snooping!" yelled Bobby, "I was just looking, I'm sorry," Bobby added quietly.

"Don't worry, it's okay," said Bobby's Daddy, motioning Bobby to come over.

Bobby smiled and ran toward his Daddy, Santa's big hat bouncing and falling over his eyes as he did, his arms stretched wide for a hug. Bobby almost ran past his daddy, as he couldn't see anything with Santa's hat pulled so low, but a big strong and gentle hand caught him and pulled him close as his Daddy laughed and said "Over here, Champ." Bobby's Daddy lifted him up off the ground -- which Bobby loved – and hugged him so that the soft hat rubbed against his Daddy's face, too.

"Oh, I love you, kiddo," his Daddy said sweetly, and held Bobby tight.

"Do you know Santa, Daddy?" Bobby asked sincerely.

"I do indeed," his Daddy said.

"Really and truly?" Bobby asked hopefully.

"Really and truly," his Daddy said, "and now, for you, it's off to bed."

And so then Bobby went to bed, pulling

the warm blankets around him, thinking "This is going to be the best Christmas of all!" As he drifted off to sleep, starting to yawn, he smiled, for he knew his dreams would be sweet and he would be dreaming of Christmas all night long.

~

FOUR-DOOR IGLOO AND WOLVES

A Poem

by Jin A Song

When the snow apocalypse
      covered the whole
City of Virginia and the sun slowly began
To dawn over the breezeless land,
My mother woke up trembling
      while raising
Her trembling voice, and gracefully threw
A ladle and a medium pot in the air to us.
A frying pan in her hand, she led

Us, two Siberian chubby wolves,
      wrapped in coats,
Hats, and gloves, with reddened eyes,
And three of us,
      poorly making howling sounds,
Crawled down the stairs
In the center of neighborhood attention.

I wondered if we, without a doubt,
Had to tear down a four-door
      Virginian igloo
Whose immobile skeletons would
      become exposed
And free by the spring sun.

My brother holding the ladle
      and I with the pot
Started to scrub the half-frosty skin,
And soft, marvelous, and purely laid
Dirt silently fell bit by bit to bring presence
Of my mother's silver van.

For two hours, we labored,
And our nearby neighbors' cars received
Unwelcoming black and white presents.
For those poor, our mercy defined
Not only the soggy snow mixed
   with our sweats
But nebulous and perplexing sound
   of the air
That might alarm the town with pairs
Of lonely hands,
In shape of unconventional foreignness.

I wondered
If they were proper gifts after all
Because the day we saw the marvels
   of the tools,
The snow, and the spirits within us
Was two days before our first Christmas
   in America.

~

TRINIDAD

A Poem

by Hamel Matthew

A memory of Christmas –
Among folks who lived to party .....
And to enjoy Holidays.
A place where –
Even for children – Christmas .....
The enjoyment of Christmas –
Entailed much work.

It was, you see –
More than anything else! –
End-of-year Renewal:

What not cleaned, varnished, painted!?!
Had to be wall-papered, repaired, refinished
Or bought, new.
Then: All the baking and cooking!!! --
'Til finally! ….. The Day arrives!!!

Meanwhile, throughout the month –
On the radio ….. Unaware of tropical
Small-island heat ….. Among others –
Bing Crosby and Johnny Mathis:
Dreaming! of a White Christmas!!!

Children!?! ….. New toys! …..
Whatever!?! – Dictated by parents' means
Or lack thereof.

Then a week of unrivaled festivity:
Visiting Carousing Eating and Drinking:
A week's Happy-hour Open-house!!!
Not to visit and partake of –
In one's immediate surroundings
Or a distant friend – was
An unpardonable insult!
As I said:

A people who lived to party!:
Who looked forward to Carnival
Six to eight weeks, later.
These festivities, everyday work
Interrupted!!! ….. Though
The day after a holiday!?!
Was also! a holiday!!!

~

ACKNOWLEDGEMENTS

Thank you to all those who created this book, including those who inspired and assisted in the publishing.

Special Thanks to:

Paul Berman
Arnold and Beverly Miller
Molly Novak
Cindy Forest
Richard Tuggle
Caroline Kremer
Kearsten Nordstrom
Joyce Kinya Kamuyu
Andrea O'Brien
Roberto Ammendola
Janlia Riley

Stacey Matthew
Amy Espiritu
Yuling Bai
Printland
& to those who write and latte
at the 18th Street Cafe

Please visit us at
www.**RememberPoint**.com

We wish you a Merry Christmas…

all year round.

Made in the USA
Middletown, DE
06 December 2016